KIDS CAN'T STOP READING
THE CHOOSE YOUR
OWN ADVENTURE® STORIES!

"Choose Your Own Adventure is the best thing that has come along since books themselves."
—Alysha Beyer, age 11

"I didn't read much before, but now I read my Choose Your Own Adventure books almost every night."
—is Brogan, age 13

"I lov happens next."
—stathiou, age 17

"Cho are so much fun to all!"
—Brendan Davin, age 11

And teachers like this series, too:

"We have read and reread, worn thin, loved, loaned, bought for others, and donated to school libraries our Choose Your Own Adventure books."

CHOOSE YOUR OWN ADVENTURE®—
AND MAKE READING MORE FUN!

Bantam Books in the Choose Your Own Adventure® series
Ask your bookseller for the books you have missed

THE YOUNG INDIANA JONES CHRONICLES™

SEARCH THE AMAZON!

BY DOUG WILHELM

ILLUSTRATED BY RON WING

An R.A. Montgomery Book

YA
WIL

BANTAM BOOKS
NEW YORK · TORONTO · LONDON · SYDNEY · AUCKLAND

RL4, age 10 and up

SEARCH THE AMAZON!

A Bantam Book/July 1994

*CHOOSE YOUR OWN ADVENTURE® is a registered
trademark of Bantam Books,
a division of Bantam Doubleday Dell Publishing Group, Inc.
Registered in U.S. Patent and Trademark Office and elsewhere.*

Original conception of Edward Packard

*Cover art by David Mattingly
Interior illustrations by Ron Wing*

ISBN 0-553-56392-0

Published simultaneously in the United States and Canada

*Bantam Books are published by Bantam Books, a division of
Bantam Doubleday Dell Publishing Group, Inc. Its trademark,
consisting of the words "Bantam Books" and the portrayal of a
rooster, is Registered in U.S. Patent and Trademark Office and
in other countries. Marca Registrada. Bantam Books, 1540
Broadway, New York, New York 10036.*

PRINTED IN THE UNITED STATES OF AMERICA

OPM   0 9 8 7 6 5 4 3 2 1

For Bradley K. Wilhelm,
who loves dolphins

AMAZON RIVER

ALTIMIRA

XINGU RIVER

SOUTH AMERICA

BRAZIL

SCALE

1 INCH = 670 MILES

WARNING!!!

Do not read this book straight through from beginning to end. These pages contain many different adventures you may have as you and your grandfather try to solve a baffling biological mystery. From time to time as you read along, you will be asked to make a choice. Your choice may lead to success or disaster!

The adventures you have are the results of your choices. You are responsible because you choose. After you make a decision, follow the instructions to find out what happens to you next.

Think carefully before you act. The unforgiving Amazon river region is the wrong place to lose your head, and you can't necessarily trust others to help you. Do you have what it takes to survive in the jungle?

Good luck!

"The pink dolphins are disappearing," your grandfather says.

"The what?"

"The pink dolphins. I'm not surprised you've never heard of them—most people haven't. They are a primitive species of freshwater dolphin. Their entire habitat is a single river basin. Over the last year or two, they've suddenly begun to disappear."

Watching your grandfather, you smile. Since he retired as a biology professor, Dr. George Coleman has written several best-selling books on solving biological mysteries. Now that he has a new mystery, his eyes are as bright as a child's.

"You mean these pink dolphins are dying?" you ask.

"We don't know," your grandfather says. "No one is finding any bodies. The dolphins are just . . . vanishing."

"So that's where you come in," you say.

"And you too, if you'll join me," your grandfather answers. "An international wildlife group has asked me to fly down and investigate. This is one species we can't afford to lose—we've barely begun to learn about them. But I'm not so young anymore, and I'll need some help. What do you say?"

The answer is obvious. "Are you kidding? When do we leave?"

Your grandfather grins. "Next week," he says. "This is a tricky part of the world. But I promise you'll never forget it."

Turn to page 2.

2

You know it's true, but right now you're thinking about what to pack. "So what part of the world is it?" you ask.

Your grandfather stands up, a triumphant smile on his face. "Brazil!" he exclaims. "We're going in search of the Amazon river dolphin."

A week later you're standing on the deck of a tall white river ship, gazing into the steamy afternoon.

It's incredible. Brown water is everywhere. The Amazon is so wide its bank is just a ragged green shimmer in the distance. "I never knew a river could be this big," you say.

"The Amazon carries more water than any other river in the world," your grandfather answers. "More than two hundred other major rivers feed into it. The Amazon river basin is home to more than a million different plants and animals. Why, half of them may still be undiscovered!"

Your grandfather sweeps his arm toward the distant jungle, and again you smile. It's funny what biologists get excited about.

"Out there is the largest forest on earth," he says. "There are fifteen hundred different birds living in this rain forest—and two thousand species of snakes . . . that we know of."

"Uh . . . that's great, Grandpa. *How* many snakes?"

Go on to the next page.

But your grandfather's on a roll. "The belt of rain forests around the equator is our world's primary treasury," he enthuses. "We cannot afford to lose it."

"Lose it? This place is huge!"

"Yes, but people are clearing the rain forest at a furious rate, mostly for cattle grazing and timber. We're losing an area twice the size of New York State each year. Once cut, it doesn't grow back. Rain forest clearing is driving up to forty-eight animal and plant species into extinction *every day."*

You're listening, but your eyes are on the water. Here and there a smooth gray back bulges up, then disappears.

"Grandpa," you whisper, "dolphins!"

"Those are the gray dolphins of the Amazon," your grandfather says. "They're much like the bottle-nosed dolphins of the ocean, only smaller."

"Is this where the pink dolphins should be too?"

"They should be—though we probably wouldn't see them," he says. "They're shy, mysterious creatures. And they're the only dolphin that hunts in the forest."

"In the forest?"

Go on to the next page.

4

Your grandfather grins. "It's true. See, each spring during the rainy season upriver, this lower Amazon overflows its banks. Miles of jungle lie mostly underwater for months. Fish swim among the trees, eating berries. Then come the pink dolphins, hunting the fish. They have long, narrow beaks and incredibly flexible, rubbery bodies, so they can actually swim through the forest!"

You're beginning to appreciate your grandfather's fascination with nature, but there's something you don't understand. "Grandpa," you ask, "if people don't usually see these dolphins, how do we know they're missing at all?"

"Well," he answers, "although most people have never seen the pink dolphins, until the recent disappearance, people could hear them."

"What do you mean, *hear* them?"

"When the *botos*—that's what the Amazon people call the pink dolphins—come to the surface, they gasp for air," your grandfather explains. "Even from a distance, people could hear them breathing. It's a very eerie sound— like a human being gasping for breath. Then suddenly the sound just disappeared from the Amazon."

"And no one knows why," you say.

"Not yet," your grandfather answers. "But we're going to see the one person who may have an idea."

Turn to page 44.

"Maybe," McLain says. "But it's no more crazy than what's happening right now in the Amazon. Quick profits are wiping out the greatest storehouse of life on earth. Many of our medicines come from rain forest plants. Did you know that? A cure for AIDS or cancer may be in here somewhere—yet it may very well be gone before we find it."

McLain stares at the ground. "But no one seemed to care, so after forty years I started to wonder why *I* should."

Your grandfather groans. You've got to get him to a doctor!

But what about McLain? Should you take him —or let him go?

If you take McLain with you,
turn to page 36.

If you let him go,
turn to page 50.

At sunrise, Zillo and a small search team arrive and take you back to Altamira. But your grandfather never returns, and neither do the pink dolphins. You'll never be sure if it was just a dream, but a part of you will always wish you had followed the *boto*'s call upstream. Perhaps the answer to the mystery was there.

Perhaps.

The End

8

Even as you sleep, you feel the firm, dry mud of the island becoming soft. It seems to swallow you, but you move easily through it. Some part of you wonders if this is a dream.

You can't see through the muddy water, but you know just where everything is around you. A strange picture appears in your mind, almost like a radar map of your surroundings.

A very large thing swims toward you, and in your mind you see it perfectly. The picture in your mind tells you this is a catfish, a catfish as big as a boat. As it swims by, your mind sees its long, trailing whiskers.

You yourself are swimming effortlessly, and as you go around the island your mind-map shows the tree roots that finger into the water from the island's edge. You see the back of the metal boat embedded in the bank. You see a school of small fish wriggling by. But it isn't *really* seeing.

How can your body flex and propel itself so smoothly like this? Bending yourself almost in two—it's easy to do—you peer through the murk, trying to see your body.

You see a soft, thick cylinder, whitish or softly pink in color. Where your arm should be, you see a broad, soft, flexible fin. You give it a flip, and you're shooting easily, powerfully across the river.

This must be a dream. *Because you seem to be a dolphin.*

Turn to page 108.

The offer seems fair. After all, any solution to preserving the Amazon must include the people of Brazil. From what you've learned today, you can help your grandfather tell the whole story.

"I'll do my best," you say.

Sylva shakes your hand. "You have courage," she says. "Good luck."

You thank her and turn to Rick, wondering how you're going to say good-bye. But Rick speaks first.

"If you'll let me," he says, "I'd like to help you find the *botos*."

You smile. "What are we waiting for?" you ask. "Let's go!"

The End

You decide the jungle is not the place for you. Rick has already risked a lot for you, but right now he's still your only chance.

"Let's run for Altamira," you say.

"Right! Here we go!"

Rick guns the motor scooter. Its little engine whines as he dodges around the Brahma cows.

You hear bigger engines catching up. You look back: The motorbikes are accelerating, spitting red dust.

"They're still with us!" you shout to Rick.

"Hang on!"

He opens the throttle to full. But there are so many cows, and the edge of the highway is so full of ruts and craters. The rear wheel slides sideways. Behind you the larger motorbikes are getting closer.

Rick stops the slide with his leg, and you're moving again. But you hear a sharp *pop* behind you—then another one. They sound like pistols . . .

The *thunk* in your back doesn't really make a sound; it just hits you like a very tiny punch. Now your back feels warm and wet.

Rick doesn't know. He's holding tight, jouncing on. There is too much bouncing—you're growing weak. You can't hold on.

You feel your hands slip from Rick's back, you see his shocked face as he turns and reaches out in vain as you fall to the Transamazon Highway.

Now you see the white legs of many cows. Then you don't see anything.

The End

Inside Rick's simple home, you sit on a plain wood chair. Your new friend starts the stove.

"I hope you like rice and black beans," he says.

"Sure. Rick, could all the land clearing in the Amazon be driving the *botos* into extinction, by drying up their habitat?"

"I don't think so—not by itself," the young Brazilian says. "Ecology is complex. When a species dwindles, there is usually more than one reason. Yes, the land clearing has affected the *botos'* habitat. There is less flooded forest for them to hunt in."

"And people say less forest means there's less rain."

"Maybe," says Rick. "But there has also been a population explosion. So many people have come, looking for their fortune. They need food. They take the fish the *botos* need. That's part of it too."

"So you don't think the ranchers are guilty?"

"I think we are all guilty," he says softly.

"Do you think the *botos* could have fled this area? Gone someplace safer?"

Rick looks at you. "That's a strange idea—but it's possible. No one really understands this creature."

Go on to the next page.

Someone bangs on Rick's door. He goes outside and has a long, whispered conversation. When he returns, his smile is gone.

"The *pistoleiros* are coming for you," he says.

"The who?"

"Gunmen. The big ranchers hire them, to do their dirty work. They want you."

"Why?"

"To take you hostage—maybe kill you. They want your grandfather to stop asking questions and leave the Amazon."

Turn to page 98.

14

Zillo is right. One look at the *botos* and you can tell they are suffering terribly.

You and Zillo remove your shirts. The gulps of dozens—maybe hundreds—of Amazon river dolphins mingle with the singing hum and buzz of millions of insects and the cries and calls of other creatures. It all pulses in your ears.

Zillo's face is set. He nods and slips into the water. You follow.

The clear water is warm and soft. It deepens as you approach the net. You breaststroke underwater, surfacing like the *botos* to gulp in a breath. Zillo's legs push him quickly, like those of a tadpole.

The net is made of some clear, modern webbing. Beyond it you see the faces of these primitive dolphins. Their skinny, toothy beaks are set in a kind of smile; their eyes are intelligent and sad. They crowd against the net—more and more of them.

Suddenly you feel what the river people feel: that these creatures are your brothers.

You've got to try.

Underwater, you pull the knife out of your pocket and saw at the webbing. Zillo holds the net. The dolphins nose toward you. It's hard not to stab their snouts, they're pushing so much.

One strand is cut through. Now another. You surface for another breath and look around. Above water, the same dark walls surround you.

From somewhere in there comes a *crack*, like a rifle shot.

Turn to page 56.

"This Colonel Costa," you ask Zillo. "What do you know about him?"

"He is the police commander in Altamira. He acts for the government."

"So what does the government want?"

"It wants business in the Amazon. It wants the big ranchers—the ones with big money. It wants them to clear more land for more cattle, to bring more big money here."

"I get it. Now, how about the Kayapo Indians?" you say. "Do you know them?"

"Sure. Why?"

"They told McLain the *boto* has found a secret place, where we shouldn't disturb him."

"That is no surprise," Zillo says.

"Why not?"

"Because outsiders have brought only trouble to the Kayapo. Their one true friend is Professor McLain. I think the Kayapo would like us all to stop disturbing them."

"So couldn't that story be a fake? Couldn't the big ranchers be paying off Costa—maybe even McLain—to tell us this story so we'll leave?"

Zillo shrugs. "Here anything is possible."

You spend the rest of the day with Zillo. You learn how life works in Altamira—how the poor *caboclos* scratch together a living while wealthy ranchers and lumber traders profit. As a shoeshine boy, Zillo is on the bottom. Yet he's as sharp as any kid you've ever known.

Late in the day you return to the guest house, bringing Zillo with you.

Turn to page 94.

16

You run and stumble through the rain forest. The light is so dim that you could easily lose this path. You don't want to do that. If you plunge into the dense jungle, you'll be hopelessly lost.

But with three *pistoleiros* chasing you, you're bound to get caught—or at least seen. And if they get a clear shot, they might take it.

Now you hear heavy breathing and the sounds of people shoving heavy branches aside. They're getting closer!

Pushing ahead as fast as you can, you stumble suddenly and slide down a muddy bank. You're at a river, or a stream. It's muddy and not very wide.

Should you cross it? What about the piranha —the small but vicious Amazon fish that travel in schools, and whose razor-sharp teeth can strip an animal clean in seconds? They're common in the Amazon, but you've heard they don't usually attack humans. Usually.

But judging by the sound, the gunmen are just a few yards behind you. You plunge into the stream and wade across. It's up to your waist, and the current is surprisingly strong. Branches and other debris bump into you. Something heavy hits your legs. Now you remember the cai-man—the Amazonian crocodile.

Sweating and gasping, you struggle to get across before you're seen—or before something grabs you.

Turn to page 113.

You shout in Rick's ear, "Why are you doing this? I thought you were my friend!"

"I am," he answers. "After the *pistoleiros* chased you, I went to see the boss rancher around here—my landlord, Sylva. I said that you and your grandfather are scientists. I said you should be allowed to search for the *boto*, because you only want to learn the truth. You only want to find the creature."

"You really said that?"

"Yes," the young rancher says. "Now Sylva wants to speak with you."

"What about the gunmen?"

"Let's hope they don't catch us first," says Rick. "Sylva was not able to contact them and tell them to leave you alone."

Do you trust Rick Neto? Should you let him deliver you to the top rancher—the *pistoleiros'* boss? What if he's lying and you're about to become a hostage—or worse?

The scooter slows to get around a horse slowly drawing a wooden cart. You could hop off and plunge into the jungle. If you're going to do it, the time is now.

*If you jump off the scooter,
turn to page 32.*

*If you go to see Sylva, the top rancher,
turn to page 101.*

Two days later, you and Zillo visit your grandfather at the clinic in Altamira. The doctor, a young Brazilian woman, has told you that he's strong enough now for visitors.

The room is dim and cool. Dr. George Coleman lies on a cot with his wounded leg heavily bandaged. He smiles.

"Grandpa! You look okay."

"I feel okay," he says. "That is, my leg feels okay. But I feel just awful about those dolphins."

You introduce Zillo. "Professor Coleman," he says, "we have an idea."

"You do?"

"You tell him," Zillo says to you. "It's really your idea."

"Okay. Grandpa, Arthur McLain has done this because he couldn't stand everyone else making money from the Amazon, and no one listening to him. I really think he loves the rain forest. And he loves the *botos*. You said yourself he knows more about the pink dolphin than anyone else."

"He does. That's right."

"So, here's our idea."

In the dim room, George Coleman listens carefully. When you've finished, a wide grin spreads across his stubbled face.

Turn to page 51.

"Okay—see what you can find out," you say. "Do the Kayapo speak Portuguese?"

"No," says Zillo, grinning. "But I speak a little Kayapo."

Nervously you step out from behind the tree.

You expect that the Kayapo women will be startled or maybe try to run away. But they don't even flinch. They don't seem to care.

Zillo speaks to a couple of the women. Without much interest, one answers. He listens, then turns to you.

"She says the men are having a big argument. The tribe is split. The ones with the professor, they have gone after the others. Those others— they are against the professor. They took your grandfather."

"Took him? Where?"

Zillo asks another question. The woman answers briefly and shrugs.

"She doesn't know for sure. But she thinks they probably took your grandfather to where the dolphins are."

"What? Do they know where the dolphins are?"

Zillo asks and the woman gives a quick wave upriver and shrugs again.

"Some secret place up the river a bit," Zillo tells you. "She says when everyone here is dying, what difference does it make?"

Turn to page 64.

At Altamira you and your grandfather step from the dock into a jam-packed, ramshackle town. The unpaved streets are choked with dust and noise.

"In this town lives the only biologist who has closely studied the *botos*," your grandfather shouts over the clamor. "I can't wait to see him again. If I can just find a taxi . . ."

But then a white jeep pulls up. A policeman waves at you to get in.

You glance at your grandfather, wondering what to do. He shrugs and climbs into the jeep, motioning for you to follow.

Turn to page 118.

This boy is sharp. There's no doubting that. He may be able to help. You decide to tell him all about your quest, and about what the old scientist and the police colonel said.

Zillo listens carefully, asking many questions. He thinks Arthur McLain's theory about the *botos* finding a secret hiding place is a little strange—but then, he tells you, the Amazon is full of strange things. "And McLain has given his life to the Amazon," Zillo says. "He is well-known and trusted here."

You know Zillo will be very helpful in your search, and you can't wait to introduce him to your grandfather.

You lead him back along the dusty road to the guest house where you and your grandfather are staying.

Turn to page 94.

24

You figure you might be in for trouble if you just start cutting the net. You decide to investigate first. But should you and Zillo go together, or should you go alone?

You hand your penknife to your Brazilian partner.

"I want you to stay here," you tell him. "There's no sense in both of us getting captured, or whatever. Hide in the leaves, but keep looking upstream for me, okay? If I can, I'll signal you. Both hands straight up means *cut the net*. Both arms straight out means *come here*. Hands on my hips means *go back to Altamira, fast*."

"Okay, partner," Zillo says.

You step from your hiding place and start to walk up the shoreline. As you move along the water's edge, you wait for the crack of a rifle shot. Every now and then a *boto* tries, unsuccessfully, to leap over the net. It's uncanny, the rubbery twisting and the fleshy pinkness of the dolphin's body.

Something appears on your left. You whirl. You're face-to-face with a Kayapo Indian. He points a rifle at you, then jerks it toward a dim path that leads through the leaves.

You start to walk. He follows, keeping his rifle trained on you.

Turn to page 116.

26

This is not like any highway you've ever seen. It's not a paved road, just a narrow gash of red dirt between high green walls, stretching as far as you can see. And the highway is full, but not of cars. Not even of people.

It's full of cattle.

Your yellow VW is caught in a slow herd of bony white cows and calves. They fill the whole highway. Way up ahead are two cowboys on horseback, wearing big white hats.

"Look at all these cows!" you exclaim.

"Sure," Angela says. "Many thousands of cows are in the Amazon. Every day the ranchers bring in more."

"I guess the ranchers are very powerful," you say.

"Yes," she says. "Around here, the big ranchers have most of the money."

"And most of the land?"

"Yes," says Angela.

Caught in this river of cattle, Angela's taxi crawls along.

"The man you are going to see, Ricardo Neto —he is a good man," she says.

"You know him?"

"I know everyone," she says, grinning again.

Turn to page 71.

You knock on Rick's door. But nobody answers. Where is he?

You look around, not sure what to do. Now you hear the sound of a small motor. It's not a chain saw this time.

You rush around the house to hide. You peek around—and see Rick on his motor scooter.

"Rick!" You rush out. He's startled at first. But then he grins and shakes your hand.

"I don't know how you got back here—but I'm glad you did," he says. "Climb on." He pats the seat behind him.

"Why?"

"So we can go to see Sylva—the boss of the *pistoleiros.*"

"What? Are you *crazy?*"

Rick laughs. "Don't worry. Sylva's my boss too." Now you're truly confused. But you hop on behind him, and he revs the scooter up and speeds out onto the highway.

Turn to page 18.

"Shoeshine!" they're saying in broken English. "Hello! Shoeshine?"

Pointing to your feet, you laugh. *"Shoe*shine? Hey, guys—I'm wearing sneakers!"

The boys laugh too, and they keep talking. Looking you over, checking you out, they chatter to each other in Portuguese, the language of Brazil. They are all wearing American-style T-shirts with the names and logos of basketball sneakers, rock bands, and sports teams.

But one boy's shirt has on it the flag of Brazil, a blue orb on a yellow diamond against a green background. That boy has been gazing at you. Now he speaks.

"I can help you," he says.

You're startled. His English sounds perfect.

"I am Zillo," he says as he leads you away from the chattering boys. "I can show you around. I can translate. Okay?"

"Yes," you say, "great. But how do you speak English so well?"

"I practice, like this—and I listen," Zillo says. "I listen very closely."

Now you understand what your grandfather said. Those who are close to the ground often hear the most.

"Zillo," you say as you walk along the dusty street among goats, bicycles, and motor scooters, "have you heard of the *boto?*"

His eyes light up. "Of course! Our *botos* have vanished. Can you find them?"

"I can try," you say. "But I need your help."

Turn to page 84.

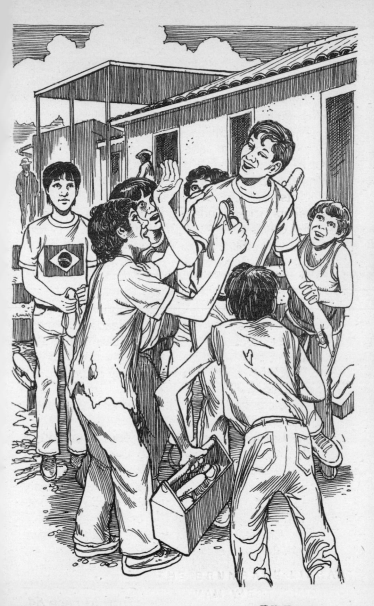

In a way, you're glad your grandfather isn't conscious. At least he won't hear the decision you've made. He's always been a strong man, and you hope he can hold out a little longer—just long enough for your plan to work.

"I've got to see this—and hear it," you tell McLain. "Being a scientist, you can understand that."

The skinny old man smiles. "Of course. Get ready to hear something you'll never forget." He says something to the armed Kayapo. They bark an order at the ceremonially painted warriors.

But the tribesmen clap their arms across their chests. They're refusing to cooperate.

Is your plan about to fail?

Hurriedly, McLain speaks with the other tribesmen. They shrug and set down their rifles.

"Money talks," McLain explains. He stoops and picks up a rifle. He points it at you.

"Just don't do anything foolish," he says.

Perfect, you think. "Hey, I'm your prisoner," you say. And, like a prisoner, you raise your arms high, straight over your head—the signal to cut the net.

You only hope Zillo is watching.

Turn to page 74.

On the dim path before you, Zillo's agile body is a shadow. You don't want to get lost, so you focus on him intently. It's a good thing too: you'd rather not wonder what creatures lurk nearby, or whether any of the dark vines looping down from the trees might actually be snakes—like the Amazon's giant anaconda, which can swallow a calf. You shudder and fix your eyes on Zillo.

Soon you see glimmering firelight ahead.

You both creep ahead to the gray trunk of a giant tree. Peering around it, you get your first look at an Amazon Indian village.

You see two simple, open-fronted structures that look like sheds. But they're very long and roofed with leaves. The structures form an "L." In the middle, cooking fires throw glimmering lights around the village.

But it isn't what you see that startles you—it's what you hear.

From within these long sheds comes coughing, sneezing, and wet, congested wheezing.

You look at Zillo. "They are very sick," he whispers.

"All of them?"

"Not all. But most. The children especially."

You hear a new sound—men arguing. Arthur McLain strides into the light with three Kayapo men. They are short and stocky, with bowl-cut black hair and American T-shirts.

McLain gestures at the Kayapo. The men go into a shed. They come back with rifles.

Turn to page 86.

Quickly you hop off Rick's scooter and dash into the undergrowth. You hear him shouting "Come back!" But you keep going.

It's late afternoon, and the rain forest seems even dimmer than usual. There's no path here. You're pushing through thick, wet tangles of vines, leaves, and branches. Suddenly you're caught in something white and gauzy—some kind of spider's web. Frantically you rip and tear at it, terrified to see what creature could spin such a big web. But you see nothing.

Finally extricating yourself from the web, you

push on, more frightened and panicked than before. But you've got no idea where you're going, and the jungle seems to be getting deeper, denser. You've got no choice but to keep going. Keep going . . . keep going . . .

Turn to page 93.

"There are two other ways you can help our investigation," he says. "You can nose around Altamira. The local folks may know a surprising amount. You might also learn something from one of the small-scale ranchers. They're not likely to sympathize with the wealthy landowners, but they may know something about their operations."

"If it's really their land clearing that's wiping out the pink dolphin," you say, "maybe the big ranchers don't want you to tell the world about it."

But your grandfather shakes his head. "I doubt that. Sure, they might have paid off the police to pressure us into leaving. But not Arthur McLain. I trust him. Arthur's a scientist."

If you make inquiries around town,
turn to page 111.

If you pay a visit to the cattle ranchers,
turn to page 66.

Suddenly an idea flashes in your head. "Well, okay," you say. "I guess we should go. But I'd really like to hear the Kayapo do this incredible song of the *boto*. We've come all this way. Could they sing it for us?"

If you can just get them to do it, everyone will be distracted. Maybe you can signal Zillo to cut the net.

McLain's eyes twinkle proudly. "It *is* fascinating," he says. "But I'm afraid if your grandfather is not rushed to a doctor now, he may die."

You look. McLain has a point. The red stain on your grandfather's bandage has spread. And he seems to have lost consciousness.

Still, if your plan works, you *might* be able to free the dolphins and still save your grandfather. Either way, you've got to choose—now.

*If you leave now,
turn to page 47.*

*If you stay to listen to the dolphin song,
turn to page 30.*

"We've got to get back," you say to McLain, "and you're coming with us."

"No," he says, standing up. "I've given my life to the Amazon. I'll end my days here."

Quickly he turns away and, like the Indians, vanishes into the rain forest.

"Should we chase him?" you ask Zillo.

"We could never find him," the Brazilian boy answers. "This is his home."

"I guess you're right. Besides, we'd better get my grandpa to a doctor—fast."

You load your grandfather into McLain's small powerboat and head for Altamira.

Your grandfather, it turns out, will be okay. Soon you're both ready to return to the States.

When the plane finally lifts you off the runway, you take one last look at the Amazon—steamy, green, and patchy with chewed-up sections of cleared land. It's so incredibly huge, stretching farther in all directions than you could ever imagine anything going.

"I don't think I'll ever understand the Amazon," you say.

On the seat next to you, a brown head turns to look out the window.

"Don't worry," says Zillo. "While I'm going to school with you in the States, we can have lots of talks about the Amazon."

You smile at your friend. "I'm glad we persuaded my grandpa to bring you back with us," you say. "Since you have no family here, we can be your family now."

The End

The image now on your mind-map is one of the river as it must have been many years ago. There are hundreds of *botos* there, swimming together and feeding in the lush, freshly flooded forest by the riverbank.

But flashing once again to your current mind-map, you remember that the river hasn't flooded into the forest this season. So each hungry *boto* has had to search far upstream for food. You only wish you knew how far.

With a flip of your tail, you surface and gulp a breath of warm air. With every one of your senses straining, you try desperately to locate the other *botos*.

Finally, very distantly, you hear something calling from upstream, beyond your hunting waters, an area your mind-map does not know.

The sound is the *botos'* call! By instinct, you swim quickly toward the unknown stream.

Even as your human mind wonders if it is safe to travel into waters outside your mind-map, the call to your dolphin instincts gets stronger and stronger. It's like magic—as if the legends about the *botos'* mysterious powers of attraction are true.

Nearing the edge of your mind-map, you send out many signals and listen carefully. From up the small stream the call comes constantly.

It is the simultaneous call of hundreds of *botos!* You've found them!

Go on to the next page.

But the dolphins sound odd now, perhaps weak or sick, and your human mind cautions you: Something is strange about this. Something's not right. *Turn back*, says your human mind.

Yet your dolphin mind only wants to go. Your two minds struggle against each other now in a tug-of-war of instinct versus intellect. Again your human mind reasons that this must be a dream. But dream or reality, you also know that you must make a choice.

*If you follow the call upstream,
turn to page 43.*

*If you turn back to your mind-map waters,
turn to page 95.*

You grab McLain's wrist with all your strength. Struggling, the two of you tumble to the ground. He strains to reach the button that will kill hundreds of dolphins.

Suddenly a bare foot slams down on McLain's wrist. He howls in pain as the device falls free. The bare foot kicks it into the water and it is gone.

You look up. It's the painted Kayapo warrior —the one who spoke.

Behind him all the other Indians have vanished. As the *botos* dashed for freedom, the Indians must have disappeared into the rain forest.

You stare up at this Kayapo. He looks down at you. There's so much you wish you could tell him—so much that you wish could have been different.

But he turns away, and now he too is gone.

The rush of escaping dolphins makes a sound like a slippery waterfall. You hear the *botos'* gasps as they gulp air and break for the open river.

You turn to see a skinny, dripping boy walking toward you. Grinning, he raises his fist in triumph. You smile too and return the salute.

Beside you, Arthur McLain slumps in defeat. He stares at the last escaping dolphins.

"They were my life's work," he says softly. "And I was ready to kill them all."

"I still don't get it," you say. "Why?"

McLain sighs.

"No use keeping the secret now," he says.

Turn to page 75.

A few minutes later, you sit in the bow of a weather-beaten but seaworthy canoe. Moonlight shimmers across the dark water. Black jungle walls rear high on both sides of the Xingu. From deep within those walls comes the steady drone of insects, punctuated by *eeps,* rustles, an occasional distant shriek, and a lot of snores.

"Just tell me what's snoring," you whisper.

"Monkeys," says Zillo.

"Oh. Of course."

As your paddle dips in the black water, you can't help wondering how you came to be here. You're paddling a canoe up a river in the Amazon, with a Brazilian shoeshine boy, in the middle of the night. You're on your way to a village full of Indians who are probably hostile.

"How well do you know the way?" you ask.

"I am a *caboclo*—I know this river," Zillo says. "I know where the Kayapo village is, and I know a path that will let us sneak up on it."

"Sneak up—on Indians? Is that possible?"

"It shouldn't be," Zillo says kind of sadly. "Not long ago the Kayapo were a proud and strong people—the eyes and ears of the jungle. But that is not so anymore."

"What do you mean?"

"You will see."

After about an hour, Zillo guides your canoe to shore. You step silently onto a sandy bank.

Zillo holds a finger to his lips and motions for you to follow as he steps into the jungle.

Swallowing your fear, you slip in behind him.

Turn to page 31.

The dolphin mind-pull is simply too strong to resist, and your instincts finally win; you follow the call. The unknown stream grows narrow, working upward. But your echoes indicate that it widens and deepens ahead—and that up there are many, many *botos*. From up there too comes the powerful attraction call.

Your dolphin mind has taken over. As you approach the wide, deep pool that is so filled with other *botos,* you do not understand the thing that stretches across the water, that you push against but cannot pass. You know only that you are on one side, shoving your beak against this thing. All the other *botos,* so many of them, are on the other side.

The attraction call still draws you, still lures you. You want to join the *botos,* to be with them all. You stay here, nosing at the net, paying little attention to the small boat that approaches you from behind. Now the boat is beside you. Something dips in the water and draws you up.

Turn to page 76.

Two days later, you sit in a swaying hammock on a much smaller riverboat, shaded under a yellow canvas roof. The boat chugs up the Rio Xingu, a big tributary of the Amazon. Your destination: Altamira, a boomtown in the rain forest.

But around here the rain forest has been burned away.

A scorched and devastated land stretches alongside the Xingu. All across the brown-red ground lie thousands of blackened, broken trees and plowed-up root clusters. Here and there rise traces of smoke.

"Some Amazon land is cleared in small patches by settlers, poor Brazilians hungry for land to farm," your grandfather says. "But these huge tracts are cut and burned by powerful ranchers who clear the Amazon to graze beef cattle. Yet the soil of the rain forest is thin. Once cleared, the ground parches and dies—it won't even grow grass for long. So the ranchers have to clear more, then more and more."

Turn to page 22.

"But why?" you ask McLain. "Why kill every last *boto?*"

"I don't want to—but I will," McLain answers. "It's your choice. Leave this place with your grandfather this minute—go to Altamira, get his wound treated, and fly immediately out of the Amazon. Or I will kill all these animals now."

"But . . . how did the Kayapo get them here? And *why?* What's this all about?"

"I will answer the first question," McLain says. "The second is our secret. You see, the Kayapo have lived side by side with the *boto* for centuries. They have loved the creature and listened to him. In their ceremonies, they sing to him. They sing the *boto*'s attraction call—the sound he uses to lure other members of his species. It's the most powerful sound the *boto* can make.

"Downriver, the dolphin's habitat is being destroyed by the clearing of the forest," McLain says. "So from here the Kayapo sang their attraction call. The *botos* came upstream. Perhaps they hoped to find a better place—if dolphins can hope. Before long, we had them all." He smiles. "I wish you could have seen it— you'd have been so impressed," he says. "But now you must leave us. You may even take our boat. Go, or else all the *botos* die."

You stare at McLain, thinking hard. You look at your grandfather. He's barely conscious.

McLain raises one finger and holds it above the detonating device. "Well?"

Turn to page 106.

You have to face it—McLain holds all the cards. And you can't let your grandpa die.

"Okay," you say softly. You sigh, casually placing your hands on your hips—the signal for Zillo to go back to Altamira.

"These men will help you get George to the boat," says McLain. He speaks to the Kayapo. Two of them put down their guns and pick up your grandfather.

You begin to walk downstream. "Remember our deal," says McLain. "Not a word to anyone, or these creatures are gone forever."

You wheel to face him. "Maybe you were these dolphins' friend once," you say angrily, "but you're their worst enemy now."

McLain shakes his head. "You'll never understand," he says. "You don't know what it's like to watch the Amazon that you love just taken away."

"I *do* know that you're not helping bring it back!" you counter.

But McLain doesn't answer.

The Indians load your grandfather into the outboard-powered boat. You start the engine and head downstream.

But where's Zillo? Did he see your signal?

Turn to page 114.

turn to page 54

You watch in amazement. Among the millions of insect species in the Amazon are fire ants, who sometimes swarm in whole colonies on floating limbs or chunks of wood. They form tight, living balls that travel on water through the forest. The ball floats until it hits something— then the fire ants instantly shoot all over whatever they've struck. And they're called fire ants because their bite has a wicked venom.

The gunman shrieks. As he staggers onto the bank, the other two men burst from the forest. They stop, horrified—then wheel and dash back the way they came.

The ant-covered man falls to the mud, rolling over and over, back into the water. You hear his agonized howl even after the current has taken him well out of sight.

You pull at your feet until with a sucking sound they come loose. You grab a branch and pull yourself out of the muck.

Now what? You could keep going along this path. Or you could follow the *pistoleiros*.

In a way, that makes sense. They're panicked. You can stay out of sight and see what they do. You might get back to the highway.

Or you might be spotted. Following the path will get you farther away from the gunmen—but deeper into the jungle.

If you trail the pistoleiros,
turn to page 90.

If you continue along the path,
turn to page 54.

50

You decide to leave McLain in the rain forest. A few days later, you and Zillo sit with your grandfather on the veranda of the Altamira Guest House. Your grandfather is going to be okay.

"Don't remember Arthur McLain as a criminal," he says. "He worked so hard, only to see much of his precious Amazon destroyed. It was just too much for him—and he never had enough friends in his fight to save this place."

"Grandpa," you ask, "is it worth it? I mean, fighting to protect the rain forest? All the power seems to be on the other side."

"Not so," your grandfather answers. "When people care about something enough to speak up and act, that's the most powerful force on earth. And you young people are tomorrow's fighters for a living world. If you don't turn the tide of destruction, in *one human generation* the world's rain forests will all be gone. So here's the big question: Do *you* think it's worth it?"

You nod. "Yes, Grandpa."

Your grandfather smiles and shakes your hand. "You'll make a difference," he says. "And what about you, Zillo?"

Turn to page 119.

"That is a terrific idea," your grandfather says. "As for my part in it, the answer is a definite yes."

"Great! Now," you ask, "how do we start?"

"Give me a few minutes," he says. From his bag by the bed, he pulls out a pen and a pad. Carefully he writes a letter. Then he folds the paper and hands it to Zillo.

"Arthur McLain never saw you, Zillo. Isn't that right?"

"Yes, sir. He never did."

"It won't alarm him to be approached by a simple Amazon boy. You bring him this letter—and this pen and paper."

"Right," Zillo says. And he's gone.

"Now," your grandpa says to you, "how about a game of gin rummy while we wait?"

"You're on."

Turn to page 87.

(Turn to page 67.)

"Angela!"

Stepping into the open, you wave her down.

Hopping out, the young woman looks you over. "You want to get into my taxi like *that?*" she asks, grinning.

"Listen, Angela—you've got to help me. *Pistoleiros* are after me. How can I get back to Altamira?"

Angela looks up and down the highway, her eyes flashing with contempt.

"Those stupid hit men—they're just boys with guns," she says. "They terrorize innocent people, hurt and kill them—for money. Everything's for money here. What did you do to get them after you?"

"We were asking questions."

"Isn't that terrible," she says sarcastically. A slow grin spreads across her face. "Well, they won't get you."

Angela strides to the front of the VW. She opens the hood.

"Climb in," she says.

You look at the cramped, empty space under the hood. Now you remember—VW Beetles have their engines in back.

"Well, I'll miss the scenery," you say. "But I might get there alive."

You climb in. Angela latches the hood down over you.

Turn to page 67.

You don't know where this jungle path is going—but it's got to lead somewhere. And any place is safer than back with the *pistoleiros*.

At least you hope so.

You're pushing vines aside, following the path in the shadowy dimness. Suddenly you hear a heavy rustling ahead of you. You freeze.

From the jungle a big, dark shape steps heavily onto the path.

You can barely see through the shadows, but the thing is the size of a Saint Bernard. It's shaggy and moves slowly. Turning, the creature spots you. You tense for an attack—but it turns back and shambles heavily into the underbrush.

You realize the creature was a capybara, a plant eater, the world's largest rodent. You remember your grandfather telling you that despite the Amazon's vast size and complexity, most of its creatures are tiny.

"The deadliest ones—certain spiders and snakes, for example—are quite small," he said. "Except for one large creature, who's the most destructive of all."

"What's that?"

"Why, the human being, of course."

Now you hear the sound of humanity—a whining sound.

It's a small engine, up ahead somewhere. Should you follow the sound? Is it a motorbike? Its revving drops, and there's a ripping sound.

What is that sound? You know you've heard it somewhere.

Turn to page 68.

"So," you begin awkwardly, "where do you live?"

"Here," says the shoeshine boy.

You look around at the crowded, dusty street. "Here?"

"Sure. Wherever I can earn a few cruzeiros, that's where I live."

"So you've got no home? No family?"

"Not like you mean," says Zillo. "But the Amazon is my home. All the *caboclos*—the river people, like me—are my family."

"But how do you survive? Just by shining shoes?"

"No—I find many ways," he says, grinning. "Sometimes I can guide people—on the rivers, even in the jungle. Perhaps I can help you. What are you looking for?"

Suspiciously, you peer at him. "How do you know I'm looking for something?"

"Everyone who comes to the Amazon is looking for something," Zillo says. "Usually it's a way to make lots of money quickly. But I can tell you are not like that."

Turn to page 23.

More cracks follow. Zillo's body jerks. Red fluid streams from him and he flails back, grabbing for the net. You start for Zillo, but he motions to you to keep cutting!

More determined than ever, you saw through strand after strand, until the small opening widens to a great tear. Dozens of dolphins push through. In an instant you're bowled over, battered, trapped underwater.

All these bodies—they're big up close, and so powerful, and they're all pushing so hard to be free. You're out of breath and dizzy. You kick

and swim hard for the surface, but you hit your head on the mucky bottom. You've swum the wrong way! You're getting dizzier. You've got to get air.

You kick with your last strength up toward the roiling turbulence at the surface. But you get caught in the surging crowd of dolphins. Flailing, you try to draw breath but gulp in water instead.

Go on to the next page.

You know it's over. You're drowning. But these beautiful, intelligent creatures—who called to you somehow, asking for rescue—they are free.

You'll never know why they were penned, nor how. But for their freedom, for these sacred creatures of the Amazon, your life seems a fair trade.

The End

"I can't let you risk any more than you already have," you say. "I'll take my chances in the jungle."

"There's a path right there," says Rick. "See it?" He points to a dark, narrow crack in the dense green alongside the road.

"Yes."

"Whatever you do, stay on that path. Don't get lost. Now go! Before they see you."

You slip off the scooter and duck into the opening in the jungle wall.

In here it's dim. There's every shade of green, every shape. Green leaves are broad and waxy, long and sharp; green vines twine around the gray trunks of trees. Looking up, you can see only an incredible complexity of green. Somewhere up there is the sky—but all you can see, way up above, is a pale brightness. From far overhead you hear the sounds of chittering birds and chattering monkeys.

Now you hear a sound you don't like at all.

From behind you comes the *burr* of several motorbikes. The *pistoleiros!* Instead of passing by on the highway, their noise stops. The bike engines are cut. There's some rustling in the underbrush. Now you hear footsteps coming toward you. Quickly.

Run! You've got to. But do you have a chance?

Turn to page 16.

Just as he swings his arms back to jump, you grab Zillo's T-shirt.

"I am sorry," he says, "but I've got to—"

"Just listen, Zillo!" you say. "Listen to me for one minute. I've got an idea. If you don't like it, you can jump. I won't stop you."

He considers for a moment.

"Please, Zillo. Those *botos* aren't going anywhere."

"Okay. I will listen."

You begin to explain your idea. When you're finished, Zillo slowly nods.

"It could work," he says. "Do you think your grandfather will agree?"

"I don't know. But he might."

"Okay," Zillo says. "Let's try it. But if your grandfather doesn't agree, I'm coming back here—with your knife."

"Deal. Now let's move!" You twist open the throttle and shoot off down the river.

You're on your way back to town. You only hope you'll be in time to save your grandfather —and that he'll go along with your plan.

Turn to page 19.

You're in the leaves, about twenty feet from the net. You look around for signs of the Kayapo, McLain, or your grandfather. But the green walls of the jungle reveal nothing.

Staring at the *botos* that crowd the water, Zillo whispers, "How can they do this?"

"I don't know. What should we do?"

"We must free the *boto*. Captured here all together, they will surely die."

"I have this," you say, reaching in the pocket of your shorts. You pull out your penknife.

"It's a good American knife?" he asks.

"It's Swiss, actually."

"Okay, Swiss is good," says Zillo. "We can slip into the water. You cut, and I will steady the net. If you get tired, we can change places."

"What if the men are watching? Someone up here has guns—we know that. Besides, shouldn't we try to scout out the situation? I mean, McLain's a scientist—and the Indians love the *boto*. If they did this, maybe there's a good reason."

"What good reason can there be to pen up the most special creature of the Amazon?"

"Maybe that's the only way to save it—to protect it," you answer.

"I cannot believe that," says Zillo. "But if you think we should find out more, then let us try."

If you and Zillo try to cut the net now, turn to page 14.

If you first investigate further, turn to page 24.

When you visit him this time, Colonel Costa leans forward over his desk.

"You're sure he went to the Kayapo?" he says.

"Of course I am," you say. "I saw him go."

Costa frowns. "Not good," he says. "Your grandfather is a famous man. If anything happens to him in my territory, it will be very bad."

"Bad? For whom—my grandfather, or you?"

Costa gives you a hard stare. "I don't think you understand how dangerous the Amazon can be. It's time you found out." He stands up. "Did your grandfather travel by boat?"

"Yes."

"Then that's how we'll travel too."

"Us? You and me? Right now, at night?"

"That's right," says Costa. "Let's go." He strides out into the moonlight.

Outside, Costa speaks quickly to a policeman, who walks away and returns almost immediately in the white jeep. As you climb in, you spot Zillo watching from across the road.

"Colonel," you say, "that's my friend—that boy, there. I'd like him to come."

Costa peers across the road. "A shoeshine boy? No. Our boat will have room only for you and me—and your grandfather. If we can find him."

As the jeep speeds toward the river, you turn back toward Zillo and shrug.

The boy gives you a salute. Somehow you know he'll be okay.

Turn to page 85.

The woman hasn't told you much, but at least the "secret place" doesn't sound too far away.

"Let's get back to the boat—fast," you tell Zillo.

Behind you, the coughing and sneezing fade into the night noises of the jungle.

These jungle sounds are like nothing you've ever heard. But they *belong* in this deep, mysterious place. It's the noise of human sickness that seems foreign and strange. You know the illnesses came to the Kayapo from outsiders—from people like you.

The boat bobs at the edge of the glimmering water.

"Why would some Kayapo be with McLain, and some be against him?" you ask. "Why would they be chasing each other with guns?"

Zillo explains. "McLain has lived here for many years. Many Kayapo have come to trust him—he has even taught some of them English. But others see him as just another outsider. Like your grandpa said, outsiders have not been kind to the Kayapo. Besides, I think they have done something with the *botos*. I think some of the Indians do not like it."

"But what would they do? And why?"

The shoeshine boy turns his sharp eyes to you. "In the Amazon, people do all kinds of crazy things," he says. "But for only one reason. For money."

Go on to the next page.

"Ah," you say. "The big green."

"Pardon?"

"It's an expression. *Big green* means big money."

Zillo is thoughtful. "Here, I think it is two things," he says. "The Amazon is the big green. Also, big green is the money people get by destroying this place. They sell the wood, they sell the creatures . . ."

"They sell the creatures?"

"The rare ones, yes. They sell the pelts to traders, or they capture them alive and sell them to zoos. It's a big business."

You shake your head and shove off into the jungle night.

Turn to page 81.

66

Your grandfather has already made contact with a nearby rancher named Ricardo Neto, and you decide to visit him. You figure it won't be as exciting as questioning the Kayapo, but maybe you can get some useful information.

In the morning your grandfather heads upriver in a small boat. You take a taxi to the Transamazon Highway.

The taxi is a dusty yellow Volkswagen Beetle. The driver is a young woman with a quick grin.

"We don't see these cars much in my country," you say.

"We still make them here," says the driver. "Most popular car in Brazil!"

"Your English is good," you say.

"Sure—because I am a taxi driver. All day, I talk to people. My name is Angela."

The cab rattles along a dirt road that seems mostly ruts and potholes, passing crowds of people and cheap buildings. Finally you turn onto the Transamazon Highway.

Turn to page 26.

It's dark in here. Your head and knees bang as the VW jolts over the road. And it's *really* hot.

At last the taxi rattles to a stop. The hood opens and, painfully stretching your limbs, you recognize the Altamira Guest House.

"Angela, you saved my life."

"No," she says. "I just drove my taxi."

"But what if they'd caught us?"

From under the seat she pulls out a small black pistol. "The *pistoleiros* leave me alone."

You whistle. "This is a tough place," you say.

"Yes. It is our frontier."

"That's what Rick said," you tell her.

"For you," Angela continues, "the Amazon is someplace to save. But for Brazilians, it is a world to conquer. It is the place where we can make something great of our lives." She spots a young boy standing at the dusty roadside, watching. She speaks to him in Portuguese. He comes over.

The boy is barefoot, dressed in a faded T-shirt and shorts.

"This is Zillo," Angela says. "He's a shoeshine boy—very bright. Speaks English nicely. He can help you find your way around here. But be careful." She smiles. "Shoeshine boys are very good at getting into trouble."

"*And* getting out of it," Zillo says, grinning.

Angela says good-bye, then hops back in the taxi and chugs away in a cloud of dust.

You turn to look at this barefoot boy. Who is he? And how can he possibly help you?

Turn to page 55.

You follow the jungle path toward the whining, ripping sound. It grows louder. Finally, up ahead, you glimpse something like a clearing.

It *is* a clearing—and that sound, you realize as you push through the last heavy leaves, is a chain saw.

Trees are down and tumbled over each other like matchsticks. In the center in a cloud of smoke, a sweating man cuts limbs from a long gray trunk. Not far away is a battered pickup.

Climbing over fallen timber, you wave your arms.

The woodcutter sees you. He cuts his engine.

You say the only thing you can think of.

"Ricardo Neto. Ricardo Neto? Do you know him? A rancher?"

Go on to the next page.

The logger wipes his forehead and nods. He grins. "Ricardo Neto—*sim*," he says, Portuguese for "yes."

He sets the chain saw down. He points to his truck and waves for you to come.

You walk, climbing over and around the logs, toward the truck. The man climbs in. You open the passenger door. The logger guns the engine and jounces along a rutted track—then turns onto a road.

You're back on the Transamazon Highway. You look quickly up and down, checking for the *pistoleiros*.

Turn to page 92.

"Ricardo was a teacher—from Rio de Janeiro, our most beautiful city. He left that lovely place and his family to come live here, with heat and dust and rain and bugs." She swats a crowd of mosquitoes.

"Why?"

"To make money," Angela says. "Brazil is a very poor country, with a lot of people. We all think the Amazon is our place to find riches. If we are very brave and work very hard, maybe we can bring a fortune back home."

"But every new person needs land—and cuts down more of the rain forest."

"Yes," says Angela.

"Then the rain forest doesn't grow back," you add.

"No. But the forest is very big."

Alongside the Transamazon Highway are stubbly patches of cleared land, some small and some very large. Cows graze on thin grass. Many huts, houses, and barns have been built.

At one small patch, Angela pulls the Volkswagen out of the stream of cattle.

"Here is the ranch of Ricardo Neto," she says. "Listen. Be careful. People know you are here."

You wonder what she means. But a smiling, friendly-looking young man is striding toward you.

Turn to page 89.

You paddle up the clear stream. It moves crookedly through the green tunnel. The foliage has closed in all around you now, so densely that the morning sunlight never reaches the water. You're paddling in murky gloom.

After a while, you begin to hear the gasping again. And this time it's not in your head.

Zillo whips around. "It is the *botos*," he says. "But . . . it is *many botos!*"

Awestruck, you nod.

Ahead, the clear stream widens and deepens. Farther up it seems to spread out, and the green walls open up. There must be a broad pool up there, like a hidden pond or lake.

And up there something is stretched across the stream. You point to it. Zillo nods and turns the canoe to shore.

Crouching, you pull the canoe into some leaves. Staying within the leaves, you creep toward the odd thing across the stream.

It's a net. It stretches mostly underwater and about six feet above, blocking the stream so that nothing can swim through—or jump over.

And the water just beyond the net is alive with large, swimming shapes, the color of pink flesh. You see bony pink backs—many of them—as they surface and slip beneath the water again.

You've found the *botos*.

And if there's a net, there must be people. Maybe people with guns.

Turn to page 61.

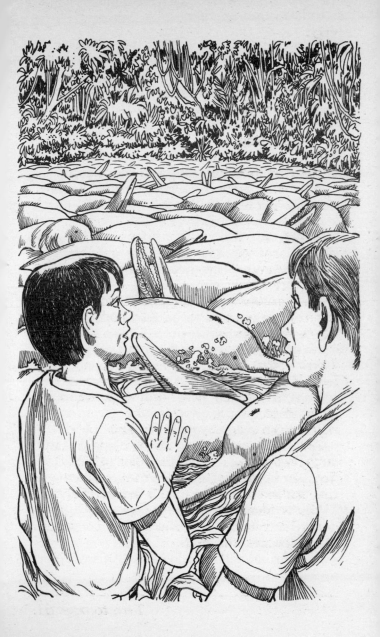

McLain holds the gun on you and the painted warriors, who stand angrily nearby. The four T-shirted Kayapo gather at the far end of this clearing.

The long pool is alive with pink dolphins, who mill and slither over each other in one fantastic crowd. The T-shirted Kayapo begin to make sounds. They make some high-pitched chirps—not really like birds. More like noisy baby monkeys. And they squawk in a way you've never heard before.

You see many *botos* turn. Their beaks emerge above the water. But they do not answer, not yet.

The Kayapos' squawking and chirping continues. The *botos* seem to be listening. You, McLain, and the others listen too. You're all looking at the dolphins and away from the net.

Now some dolphins begin to respond. In a few moments, chirps and squawks are coming from all across the pool—from dozens, even hundreds, of long, narrow beaks.

Now the Indians begin a different sound. It's more like singing, though not like human singing. Their slow-rising, high-pitched wailing comes from somewhere deep in their throats.

At first the plaintive sound is soft and sad, but slowly it grows until the Indians are wailing loudly. Their voices waft over the pool of *botos*. This is definitely the strangest sound you've ever heard—this attraction song of the Amazon river dolphin.

Turn to page 91.

"I've spent forty years in the Amazon," the old scientist says. "I've watched people come in here and clear the forest for cattle, take away its lumber, steal its precious creatures—and make fortunes doing it. What have I got? Nothing.

"The Kayapo are dying from the diseases we have brought. They have no power and no doctors, because they have no money. My scheme was going to give them money—lots of it. And me too. Why shouldn't I grow rich from the Amazon, like everyone else?"

"But how?"

"Simple," McLain answers. "With all the pink dolphins confined to this one pool, most would have died—but not all. A few would have survived."

"Then what?"

"If there were only, say, a dozen pink dolphins left in the world, imagine what the richest aquariums would have paid for each one of those."

"But that is crazy," Zillo says.

Turn to page 5.

Strange hands grab you, lifting, and suddenly you are wide awake. You get a glimpse of a wide pool that is surrounded by trees and seems to be filled, crowded with pale shapes. Twisting and writhing, you see the two muscular Kayapo Indians whose hands grip your arms and legs.

Arms and legs! You're human! The dream is over—if it *was* a dream.

In a panic you whip your head around and spot Arthur McLain watching on the bank! Why doesn't he do something?

"Dr. McLain!" you scream desperately.

But McLain just turns away as the Indians heave you over the long net that blocks the big pool in which all the *botos*—some alive, many dead or dying—are imprisoned.

The curious dolphins crowd around you, their fleshy bodies pressing against yours. Not meaning to, they push you down, under the water. You push and push back but there are too many of them. The air is expanding, pressing in your lungs. You don't have the dolphins' ability to stay under for so long. You can't hold out . . .

Everything goes pale, like the pale bodies all around you. You become calm, and as you fade from consciousness, you accept your fate. The Indians and McLain found you asleep on the island, brought you here, and have now disposed of you. Your body is lost among the crowd of drowning dolphins, never to be found. You'll never know why on earth they were all here.

The End

"What?" You turn to the armed man. "You *shot* him? Where is he?"

You step toward the T-shirted Kayapo. He points the rifle at your stomach and speaks loudly.

From the jungle steps Arthur McLain. "So you've found us," McLain says softly. "I wish you hadn't."

"Where is he? Is he okay? Why did they shoot him?"

"Your grandfather is wounded," says McLain. "When he saw the dolphins, he became . . . difficult for these men to control."

You stare at McLain. He looks calmly back at you.

"Now I get it," you say. "*You* did this. You're an expert on these dolphins—only you could have lured them all here."

But McLain shakes his head. "No," he says. "Only these Kayapo have that wonderful ability. I merely convinced them it was the intelligent thing to do."

"What's so intelligent about this?" you demand. "Won't all these dolphins die?"

"That," says McLain, "is up to you."

Two more Kayapo come out, carrying your grandfather. His leg is wrapped in a blood-soaked T-shirt. He looks pale and bewildered.

Go on to the next page.

"Arthur," he whispers, "how can you do this? You're a scientist!"

"It's too late for that," McLain says. From his pocket he produces a small unit, like a calculator.

"This pool is wired with explosives," he tells you. "It's our precaution against anyone interfering with our plan. You see, if I push this button, every last Amazon river dolphin on earth will die."

Turn to page 46.

"The *boto* is the Amazon's most legendary creature," the old biologist begins. "People say he comes to humans in their dreams. They believe he can lure a dreamer into his underwater world."

"I've heard that," your grandfather says.

"Well, no people are closer to the *boto* than the Kayapo Indians, a tribe that lives near here. I'm convinced they can actually communicate with the *boto*. You see, the dolphin navigates by making sounds and listening to the echoes. It's a kind of sonar—quite remarkable. The Kayapo have learned to mimic the dolphins' sounds.

"But there are not many Kayapo left," McLain goes on. "And they believe that, like themselves, the *botos* cannot survive in the Amazon much longer."

"Why not?"

"Because of all this land clearing. The river basin is drying up," McLain explains. "The vegetation holds the rainfall in the ground. With the plants gone, the rainfall simply runs into the river. That means less flooded forest. The *boto*'s habitat is shrinking fast."

"I knew the dolphin population had declined," your grandfather says. "But why this sudden disappearance?"

"The Kayapo say the *boto* has retreated to its last hidden refuge," McLain answers. "It may survive there, in small numbers—but only if it is left alone. If we disturb them, the last *boto* will die."

Turn to page 112.

You're paddling up the Rio Xingu in darkness. "Only one problem," says the Brazilian boy.

"What's that?"

"We have no idea where we are going. Also, it is dark. Also, the Kayapo have guns, and we do not."

"That's not one problem," you say. "That's three."

"Right," Zillo says, chuckling.

"So would money have anything to do with the pink dolphin?"

"I'm not sure," Zillo muses. "But the more scarce an animal is, the more valuable. Suddenly, the *boto* has become very scarce."

You paddle for a long time, pondering this strange situation.

Finally, dawn begins to break. Wispy mist hugs the dark water. Along both riverbanks the high walls turn from black to green. They're so dense you can see only dimness within. It's like paddling through a leafy tunnel, and only the very top is open to the sky.

The night sounds give way to the creatures of day. You hear insect hums and buzzings, bird calls, coos and caws. You hear strange belches, screeches, growls, and a sudden, maniacal howl.

You grab Zillo's sleeve.

He grins. "Howler monkey," he says.

"Uh, right," you answer. "That's what I thought."

Then you hear something else—a sound that chills you to the bone.

Turn to page 110.

You dive to the bottom of the boat. But you realize this won't do any good—they'll shoot right through the aluminum. You've got to get out of here!

With one hand you reach out and grab the tiller of the outboard motor. With the other you reach for the throttle, opening it up full. The boat kicks out into a wide, high turn, then lurches ahead. You wait for the next shot.

But it doesn't come. The gun, or guns, on-shore are silent.

Still you keep your head down. You keep the throttle open. Something bumps against the boat. A log? You look over the edge, but you can't see anything.

You're moving upriver, away from town, in the middle of the night. You've got no idea where the Kayapo are. Was it the Indians who shot Costa? Is that what happened to your grandpa?

Your mind is whirling with all this when the boat rams into something hard. There's a cracking sound. The motor struggles, then dies.

You raise your head. You've hit some kind of island. The boat has dug itself deep into mud, roots, and branches. Climbing out, you can't push it free. It's hard to see in the dark.

It's a tiny island—just a few trees and that's all. But the ground is dry, and you feel safe here. You decide to lie down.

Your brush with death has left you exhausted, and you fall into a deep sleep.

Turn to page 8.

Zillo grabs your hand excitedly. "Okay, we are partners!" he says. "Like in a detective movie. We are on the case!"

"Okay!" You can't help smiling too as you dodge a wooden cart piled high with bulging sacks. "So what do you know about the *boto?*"

"I am a *caboclo*—one of the river people of Amazonia," Zillo says. "We are poor people, but we love the rivers, and we love the forest. The *boto* is the soul of our world. He is very intelligent, this creature—he knows what people are doing to the Amazon. Cutting it and burning it. Less forest every year, and so less rain. The rivers are shrinking. Where can the *botos* go?"

"We met a scientist who says the *botos* have gone somewhere upriver, to a secret hiding place," you tell him.

Zillo frowns. "Who says so?"

"The American, Arthur McLain. Do you know him?"

"Oh, of course. All people in Altamira do."

"What's he like?"

"He is a strange man," Zillo says, "but he loves the Amazon. He has spent his life here. All other people from outside, they come here a short time, grow rich and leave. But the professor, he is old now, and still poor."

"He met us with Colonel Costa," you say. "They told us we should go home. It seemed odd to me, that a scientist would tell us to give up a search for knowledge."

"Yes," says your new friend. "That is odd."

Turn to page 15.

But what about you? Is this safe? Can you trust Costa?

You're not sure.

The outboard motor hums as you and Colonel Costa move up the Xingu in an aluminum boat. Between the dark walls of trees, the moon casts a pale wash of light across the water.

"Are the Kayapo really dangerous?" you ask.

"Sometimes," says Costa. "It's hard to tell what the tribe will do. Except for Professor Mc-Lain, they have learned not to trust outsiders."

"So they might not have liked it when my grandfather came."

"Maybe not. But they usually don't hurt strangers. They just send them away. That's why I'm surprised that your grandfather did not return. The Kayapo have been acting strange."

"Just lately, you mean?"

"In recent weeks, yes."

"How are they acting strange?"

"We have reports that they are quarreling. I have even heard a rumor that they have acquired weapons."

"Weapons? You mean like guns?"

"Like guns, yes."

"Is that illegal?"

"No, but the Indians do not normally have them. As I said, I am concerned."

Beside you the dark walls rise thickly to the tallest treetops, a hundred feet up in the moonlight. The jungle is so thick and dark. Someone could be watching and you'd never know.

Turn to page 96.

Rifles in hand, McLain and the Kayapo men head toward the river. In a few moments an outboard motor surges to life. You hear its low drone as the boat chugs up the Xingu.

"At least we know they've gone upriver," you say.

You stare into the village. Women emerge from the shelters and quietly move about. You can't get over all the sounds of sickness—it's as if every Kayapo has a terrible cold. As they do their nighttime chores, some women double over in coughing fits.

"Looks like the men are all gone," you whisper.

"But the professor left with only three," Zillo answers.

"Some of the others may be sick," you say.

"Maybe—but not all."

Right now, the health of the Kayapo is the least of your concerns. "I want to follow those guys upriver," you say.

"But they have a motor."

"We can follow the sound. And if they use those guns . . . we'll hear those too." You shudder at the thought. "But I don't get it. If *they* don't have my grandpa, who does?"

"Why don't we ask in this village?" Zillo suggests. "Women and sick people will probably not harm us."

"Probably?"

"You are in the Amazon," the boy says. "No matter what you do, there is danger."

Turn to page 21.

The next day you're sitting on the porch of the Altamira Guest House. Your grandfather has been discharged from the clinic, and he sits in the wicker chair beside you.

A familiar canoe slides into view, coming down the Xingu. Paddling it is a brown-haired boy in a green T-shirt.

"Here's our gutsy courier," your grandfather says.

Zillo hops up the stairs. He hands you a letter.

You can't wait to read it. "What did he write?" you ask.

"I do not know," Zillo says, grinning. "I can speak English, but I cannot read it."

You hand the letter to your grandfather, who unfolds it and begins to read.

"Uh-oh," Professor Coleman says. "I don't like how this begins. McLain writes, *'Dear George: When I read your letter I became very angry. Everyone has a scheme to profit from the Amazon. Everyone! All these years I have watched people rip easy riches from this world that I love. I could not stand it anymore. And now, from you—another scheme! I was furious!'*"

Your heart sinks. Has your plan failed?

Turn to page 103.

"Hello! I am Ricardo Neto," says the young man. "Call me Rick."

You introduce yourself.

"I admire your grandfather greatly," Rick says. "You know, I was a teacher of biology— and English—in Rio. I love science. But now I am here. This is my place."

He sweeps his arm across a modest square of scraggly grass and skinny cows.

"Actually, it's not mine yet," he says. "The big ranchers own it. I rent it. But if I'm successful, someday I may own it."

"You must miss your family," you say.

"Oh, very badly. But I am making money to send home. Someday I will make them very proud."

As he shows you around his patch of cleared forest, you realize Rick Neto is a really nice guy. You also notice that the grass is part green, part brown.

"Will this grass keep growing for your cows?" you ask.

Rick frowns. "I don't know," he says. "When the forest is cleared, the soil dries too quickly." Changing the subject, Rick brightens. "You are on a search, I understand, for the mysterious pink dolphin."

"That's right," you say. "Could we talk? I'd just like to ask you a few questions."

"Of course," Rick answers. "Come inside."

As you follow, you see the young rancher glance nervously back toward the road.

Turn to page 12.

You figure that the *pistoleiros* will head back toward civilization, so you decide to follow them. That means crossing the stream again. Taking a deep breath, you plunge back into the muck.

You look around anxiously for floating things. You search for the red eyes of a caiman. But the water seems safe for now, and you cross the stream without incident, breathing hard.

On the path in the jungle dimness there's no sign of the gunmen. You walk carefully, listening hard.

Now you hear the gunning of small engines ahead. The motorbikes! From the sound of them, the *pistoleiros* have headed for Altamira.

That might not be good. Can you get back to town without them spotting you?

For now, you've got to go on.

You follow the path. Before long you see pale light through the trees. Pushing out, you find yourself looking up and down the Transamazon Highway.

The endless crowd of cattle is finally gone. Here a truck jounces into and out of a pothole; there a man leads a donkey pulling a cart.

And bobbing down the road comes a dusty yellow Volkswagen.

Turn to page 53.

But this time the *botos* do not answer. They turn from the Indians and swim away.

McLain looks confused. The T-shirted Indians keep singing. Over and over they repeat the call. But still the *botos* do not respond.

The Kayapo warrior who spoke to you before now turns to face McLain. In a fury, he cries, "They no longer listen. They *do not listen!* Do you know what this means? Our water brothers no longer trust our song. The bond between us has lasted for hundreds of generations, and now we have broken it. All because of you and this sickness of money!"

He lunges for a rifle on the ground. But McLain quickly aims his gun at the Indian.

"No!" you shout. "Don't do it!"

But the painted Kayapo grabs and raises the rifle. McLain's finger presses his trigger.

Both men freeze as a strange, rushing sound comes from the netted end of the pool. You, McLain, and the Indians whirl around to see *botos* breaking through the net. Dozens of them are furiously funneling through the net and shooting down the stream to freedom.

Zillo did it! The plan worked!

McLain drops his gun and yanks the detonator from his pocket. Hundreds of dolphins are still in the long pool, all pushing for their freedom. He could still blow most of them up.

You can't let him do it!

You leap for McLain's hand. His finger jabs for the button.

Turn to page 41.

This logger doesn't even know you, but he's stopped work to give you a ride. Some people help each other in the Amazon, you're thinking. And some people kill each other. Your pulse quickens as you realize this man could do either.

There's no sign of the *pistoleiros*. But will Rick's place be safe? Did they see him with you?

Another chilling thought hits you: Maybe it was Rick who informed the *pistoleiros* in the first place. Maybe he was only pretending to help you.

The truck pulls up to Rick's little ranch. Should you get out?

You've got to trust your instincts. And your instincts say Rick Neto is okay.

You thank the logger. He grins, his face streaked with sweat and dirt. He waves and guns the pickup's engine, blasting you with red dust.

Turn to page 27.

You never emerge from the rain forest. No one learns what happened to you. Were you bitten by a fer-de-lance, perhaps the world's deadliest snake?

Although your mission to save one part of the Amazon fails, in a very real way you, yourself, become part of the Amazon rain forest.

In this heat and humidity, everything that dies decomposes quickly and is absorbed and recycled into the complexity of living, growing things. So it's not unusual that your body is never found.

Besides, with about two million square miles of rain forest to cover, it's doubtful anyone even looked.

The End

Late that night, you and Zillo are sitting outside the hotel. You are worried. Sunset has come and gone and your grandfather still hasn't returned.

"Maybe he has just been delayed," the boy says.

"No—it's not like him," you say. "Something's happened. Maybe somebody has done something to him—or kidnapped him. I've got to find my grandfather, Zillo."

"If you wish to visit the Kayapo Indians, I can get a boat," Zillo says.

"We might be putting ourselves in danger. Maybe I should try to find Arthur McLain. He knows the Indians best."

"I can take you to his place. Or what about telling the police?"

"I don't know if I trust Colonel Costa," you say. "He wanted us to end our investigation."

"Perhaps he knew your grandfather might be in danger," Zillo says. "Listen, Colonel Costa is a very powerful man. If your grandfather is missing, he should know."

"I guess so," you say. "But I wish I knew who's on our side around here—if anybody is."

If you try to find Professor McLain, turn to page 117.

If you report your grandfather's disappearance to Colonel Costa, turn to page 62.

With all your strength, you force the *botos'* call from your mind.

As you swim back to the deep water, you feel no more conflict or sense of danger. There's only the fantastic, three-dimensional mind-map of all the water around you, up and down the river.

Looking at the map, you are again reminded how much the landscape of the river has changed. It's difficult for your human mind to accept this, but you do your best.

But you cannot accept the loneliness. Dolphins are very social creatures, and you cannot live without other *botos,* without their friendship and play, without the feel of their bodies.

Although the water is warm, you feel a chill of emptiness. You are alone in a world you don't fully understand. For the first time, your human and *boto* minds find common ground—loneliness.

You swim aimlessly through the water, staring at the submerged tangles of giant roots. They move slightly with the current, like branches in a soft breeze . . .

You don't know how long you've been staring at the moonlit trees of your small island, but you're awake now, stretched out in the sand next to the wrecked boat. You move your arms and legs slightly and take a deep breath. You're human. And you're okay. Relieved, you let yourself drift back into a deep, dreamless sleep.

Turn to page 7.

Suddenly Costa speaks. "I am glad you are looking for the dolphins."

You stare at him in disbelief. "You?" you ask incredulously.

"Yes," he answers, staring upstream. "It is strange, I know, since I am the one who asked you to give up the search. But lately I have seen them in my dreams, these soft creatures with their strange, sad smiles. There are many of them, close together. And they are looking at me . . ."

He stops and turns back to you. "It's almost as if they are trying to communicate with me. To tell me something. I wish I knew what. Each night, I hope they will appear again, and that this time they will tell me—"

Crack! Crack!

The sharp, quick sounds come from somewhere onshore. Costa falls backward; he makes a funny noise. Something dark spreads across his khaki shirt. He stands up, drawing his pistol and looking toward shore. There's another *crack!* and, as if in a slow-motion dream, Costa falls backward, out of the boat and beneath the brown water. The ripples from his body disappear. He is gone.

You feel like you're in a dream too. You expect to blink and Costa will be back; but there is another *crack* and two bullet holes open in the aluminum boat, one on each side.

Whoever they are, they're trying to kill you too.

Turn to page 83.

You swallow hard. "What should I do?"

"I can't let this happen to you," Rick answers. "You have come for science. Come on, I'll take you."

"Where?"

"Back to Altamira. The police are there—the *pistoleiros* will not dare try to harm you in town. Out here it is outlaw country."

"This is like the Wild West," you say.

"Right," Rick answers. "The Amazon is our frontier." He hustles you out a side door and onto his motor scooter. The highway is still choked with cattle, so the scooter struggles along the edge.

"What kind of cows are these?" you ask.

"Brahma cows. From India." Rick has been checking the highway ahead and behind. "They're behind us!" he says suddenly.

You look back and see three young men wrestling motorbikes around the cattle in gusts of dust.

"Why are they doing this?" you ask.

"The ranchers don't want your grandfather to tell the world what's happening to the rain forest. Not right now," Rick says. "They want to make their fortunes first."

"Why do you say *they*, Rick? You're a rancher too."

You see his shoulders tense.

Go on to the next page.

"I know," he says. "But I do it only for my family. Now listen. I can try to outrun them and get you to town."

"If they catch us," you ask, "what will happen to you?"

"I'll lose everything. These guys are working for my landlord—the boss rancher," Rick says. "But I'd risk it—your search must go on! Or if you prefer, you can slip into the jungle now."

You don't know the first thing about jungles, and you get the feeling this one is no place for beginners. But you and Rick may both be safer if you split up.

*If you stay with Rick and
make a run for town,
turn to page 10.*

*If you slip into the jungle,
turn to page 59.*

You decide to stick with Rick. You've got to trust him, because right now, he's all you have.

The scooter turns onto a long, narrow road and pulls up at a large house with a wide porch beside the river. Some young men lounge on the porch. They're dressed in slick city clothes, like the *pistoleiros*.

You are taken to a shady living room. On a wicker chair sits a slender blond woman.

"This," says Rick, "is Sylva."

Middle-aged but athletic, Sylva has a soft voice and an aristocratic manner. "I'm so pleased to meet you," she says, extending one hand.

Could this be the woman who wanted you killed? She is elegant, yet there is a steeliness in her green eyes. You draw a deep breath.

"My grandfather is a writer about science," you say. "We are here to search for the pink dolphin—that is all. We mean no harm to you."

"But you *can* harm us," she says. "Millions of dollars, and many people's dreams, are being invested in the Amazon. Your grandfather's book can bring us much trouble. Outsiders—people who want to save the rain forest—will come to stop our work, to kill our dreams."

You nod, even as your face reddens with anger. "But what about the creatures of the Amazon, and the native people? They have no money and power here. Why shouldn't we tell their story—before you wipe them out?"

There is silence. You wonder if those indignant words will be your last.

Turn to page 107.

102

"If the professor and the Kayapo could pen up all the last *botos*," you say, "they could sell them to zoos and aquariums. They'd make money. A lot."

"And if they are all penned up in a small place," says Zillo, "most of the *botos* will die, making the few survivors even more valuable."

"It's a sad thing about endangered species," you say. "The fewer there are, the more some people want them."

"But the professor is known as a good man," Zillo says, shaking his head. "He has worked in the Amazon all his life."

"Maybe he's just been here too long. Maybe he got sick of everyone else getting rich. You said yourself he was poor. Maybe it all finally got to him."

Zillo stands up in the boat. "I cannot let this happen," he says.

"Zillo—wait!"

"No—I am sorry. You take care of your grandfather. I must free the *botos*."

You've got to stop him. He'll be killed!

Turn to page 60.

Your grandpa reads the rest of the letter aloud: " *'But then,'* McLain writes, *'I began to think more about your idea. I realized that you are right—you and I could write an excellent book about the pink dolphin. The creature is so intelligent, so mysterious, and so legendary in the Amazon. People all over the world might find such a book fascinating. And in telling the boto's story, we could tell the world what is happening here in the Amazon —and why everyone must care.*

" *'So, George, it is with great pleasure that I accept your offer. I hope our book finds many readers—and, frankly, I hope it makes a great deal of money. In any case, you have rekindled my deep devotion to saving this most precious earth and its creatures—so let's get to work! In gratitude, Arthur McLain.'* "

Your grandfather looks up, a tear of joy glistening on his cheek. "Nice job," he says to you —and to Zillo.

"But what about the dolphins?" you ask.

"He doesn't say."

Go on to the next page.

You slump back in your chair. What if this was all just part of McLain's plan? But then something makes you sit bolt upright.

"Do you hear that?"

"Hear what?"

"Listen."

From the distance comes a rushing sound, like many people gasping.

"I hear them," says Zillo.

"So do I," says your grandfather.

This time you know the sound of the *botos* is not coming to you in some dream, like before. This time, it's real. The *botos* are free. And they're swimming—hundreds of them—back down the Xingu.

They're coming home.

The End

You've got to keep McLain talking while you think.

"Why are these Kayapo dressed this way?" you ask, pointing to the painted Indians. "And why did they grab my grandfather?"

"They do not agree with our project," McLain coolly answers. "They hoped your grandfather would help expose me to the outside world. Obviously, I could not let that happen."

The painted Kayapo speaks again. "McLain has betrayed us," the warrior says. "We trusted him, and he talked our people into deceiving the *botos*. They did it for the one thing that has destroyed our world—money."

You turn to McLain. "How does money come into this?"

"That's our secret," he says.

"Okay. Say we do leave. What's to prevent us from telling the world about this?"

McLain holds up the detonator again. "This," he says, smiling.

Turn to page 35.

But Sylva nods. "You are right—we know that. The natives of the forest, both human and animal, must have a place here too. True, there are some ranchers with no regard for this precious balance. But do not think that we are all like that."

You nod and try to swallow. But your mouth is dry. Sylva is tough; she wants something from you. But what is it?

"I'm asking you to understand what the Amazon means to us," the boss rancher says. "When you tell the story of the *boto*—whatever you find it to be—do not make the Brazilian people into scapegoats or villains. To see each other as enemies—that is not the answer."

"You see, we *need* the Amazon," Rick says. "We are a very poor country, and it is an incredible natural resource. We cannot make it all into some big park. But we *can* learn to tend it, like a garden, before it is gone."

Sylva nods. "Include our side in your story," she repeats. "I ask only this. If you agree, I will provide you safe passage back to Altamira. And if you or your grandfather need help, just ask."

Turn to page 9.

108

Although your human mind is still conscious, you allow your dolphin instincts to take over.

A dolphin doesn't think about things the way a person would. It's very peaceful, but you feel very aware. At every moment, your *boto* mind takes in a vast amount of information and places it within the incredible three-dimensional map in your head.

Your mind-map can show you the river, all the way from one side to the other, and even a long way upstream. You can "see" the fishes, small and large, and you can see a floating log, the tangled roots, a crocodile lurking in the shallows. You see everything—yet your eyes barely penetrate the murk.

How is this possible? Your human mind wonders.

Only now do you realize you're constantly giving out sounds. From your beak flows a steady series of noises. These spread through the water and rebound off the fish, the roots, the crocodile. The sounds return to fill in the detailed, shifting picture in your mind.

Your human mind remembers learning in school about sonar, a technique some animals use to recognize their surroundings underwater or in the dark.

But now a very different picture appears on your map, and your dolphin mind reminds you that something is terribly wrong.

Turn to page 38.

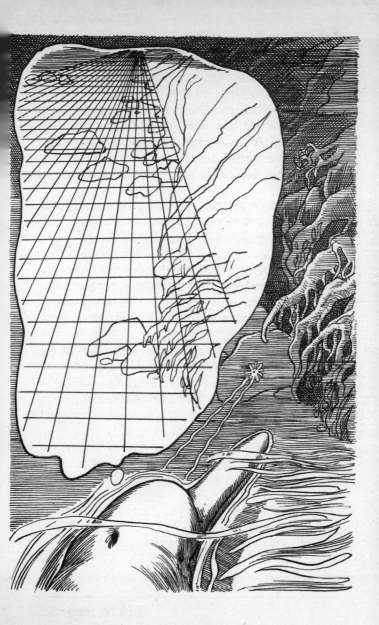

Far off to your left somewhere, you hear the sound of breathing.

It sounds like a crowd of people, everyone gasping for air. But you can't see anyone.

What could it be? You sit frozen, listening. You can't tell how far away these people are—it's as if their sound is coming to you in a dream.

"Do you hear that?" you whisper.

Zillo turns back to you. He cocks his head.

"What?"

"That sound—*that*. Like people breathing."

He pauses. Now he shakes his head. "No. I hear nothing like that."

It *is* like a dream. The sounds aren't out there. They're in your mind. How is this happening?

On the left, a small tributary flows into the Rio Xingu. This stream pulses in from the forest, its waters clear until they're absorbed in the muddy river.

You somehow know the gasping sounds are coming from somewhere up that stream.

"Zillo," you say. "The *boto*—what does he sound like?"

"He sounds like a man drawing a breath—distant, but also near. Very strange sound."

"Zillo. We've got to go up this stream."

Turn to page 72.

You decide to make some inquiries around town. Early the next morning, your grandfather is ready to go. It's still cool as you walk with him to a wooden dock at the riverbank. A battered aluminum boat awaits.

"Where are these Indians," you ask, "the Kayapo?"

"They're up the Rio Xingu a few miles," your grandfather says. "I'll be back before nightfall. Now find out what you can," he adds, lowering his voice. "Remember, those who are closest to the ground often hear the most."

"I'm not sure what that means."

He smiles. "Go nose around. You'll see." He shakes your hand and steps into the boat. He yanks the starting cord, and the little outboard motor sputters to life.

"See you at sunset," your grandpa says as the boat swings into the slow-moving Xingu. You wave and turn back toward the town.

But suddenly a crowd of a half dozen boys comes charging up. In a flash, they've got you surrounded.

The boys all talk at once. Each one clutches a wooden box that's a little bigger than a shoe box.

Turn to page 28.

Colonel Costa speaks up. "You see, pursuing this creature can only do it harm."

"Yes," McLain says. "It would be best for you to just return home."

A few hours later, disheartened by what McLain has told you, you and your grandfather sit in silence on the porch of the Altamira Guest House. Across the river is a scraggly remnant of the jungle.

Finally you break the silence. "Do you believe that story?" you ask. "Could the last pink dolphins have found some secret place to hide from the world?"

"Well, I've heard strange Amazon tales that turned out to be true," your grandfather says. "But I'm not about to just accept this one and leave." He gazes at the sunset. "Tomorrow," he says, "I'm going to visit the Kayapo."

"I can't wait," you say.

Now your grandfather looks down. "I don't want you to come," he says.

You are crushed. "But Gran—"

"This tribe can be dangerous," he interrupts. "Outsiders have done them no favors."

You wonder what that means.

Turn to page 34.

The muddy water surges against you, and the bottom of the stream is slippery, but you make it across. You step onto the brown mud on the other side—and your sneakers are swallowed up. Your feet have sunk up to the ankles.

You're stuck.

The first of the *pistoleiros* bursts from the jungle on the other side.

"Alto!" he shouts in Portuguese. *"Alto!"*

"I guess that means stop," you murmur.

He's a young man in jeans and a shiny, stylish nylon jacket. He's pointing a pistol at you. He shouts behind him. From back along the jungle path, there's an answer.

You're caught! If you weren't stuck, you could bolt for the jungle. But you can't move.

You raise your hands.

Still training his gun on you, the *pistoleiro* starts wading across the stream. He too is surprised at its depth and struggles to keep his balance.

He's midway across when you notice a small log floating downstream. Something looks very odd about it. There's a strange, dark ball formed around a large knot in the log. It's kind of fuzzy—as if it's solid but somehow not.

On the quick current, the log floats right to the *pistoleiro*. The instant it hits him, the dark ball explodes: a million dark specks flash from it up the gunman's body, and he starts to scream.

He's covered with ants!

Turn to page 49.

114

You ease the boat into the tunnel of trees and head downstream. But you see no sign of Zillo.

Where is he? Will he try to cut the net after all? You listen for the sound of rifle shots—or of an underwater explosion.

Instead you hear the weird sound of the trapped *botos,* gasping and gulping back in their pool. There are also the mingled noises of the rain forest, which looms in green shadows all around you. And now there is a splashing sound, like something very large swimming toward you.

You shudder, peering all around. Is it a caiman, the Amazonian crocodile? Beside the boat, you see water bulge up, and now a brown head.

You're looking into Zillo's dancing eyes.

"Hi," he says.

"Whoa—am I glad to see *you.* Climb in before a crocodile gets you."

You help Zillo into the boat.

"Is this your grandfather? Is he okay?"

"I hope so. We've got to get him to a doctor."

"I know a good one," Zillo says. "Why didn't we cut the net?"

"The professor had the whole pool wired with dynamite. He would have killed all the *botos.*"

Zillo whistles. "Why? Is he crazy?"

"Maybe a little. I'm not sure. Hey—wait a second." You're remembering something. "What was that you said about people capturing rare creatures around here?"

His eyes widen. He says, "Do you think . . . ?"

"I think we've just solved the mystery."

Turn to page 102.

The armed Kayapo steers you through the forest. You emerge in a big clearing at the edge of the wide pool. Hidden by jungle, the long pool is totally full—weirdly, amazingly full—of dolphins. Packed in like big, pink, soft sardines, they mill about helplessly, sliding over each other, crowding and straining desperately at the net.

Some dolphins are dying. They've pushed themselves up on the mud along the shoreline. Some are already dead.

In this clearing stand three more armed Kayapo. They're all wearing American-style T-shirts and athletic shorts. These men are guarding a group of half a dozen more Kayapo who are dressed quite differently—as if for war, or ceremony.

The Indians under guard are shirtless. Their chests are painted with streaks of dark blue, their faces with orange and red designs. They wear bands of colored shells around their necks and upper arms. Circling their black, thick, bowl-cut hair are headdresses of orange and black feathers.

You turn to one of the T-shirted Kayapo. Pointing to the painted warriors, you say, "Did these guys kidnap my grandfather?"

The T-shirted Kayapo nods.

"Where is he?" you ask.

But one of the painted men answers. "The old man is hurt," he says. "These men shot him."

Turn to page 78.

Something about Colonel Costa made you uneasy. And Arthur McLain is your grandfather's old friend, so you decide to look for him, instead.

In the dark night, Zillo leads you through the streets of Altamira to McLain's laboratory.

When you see it, you're shocked.

You expected a modern, well-equipped scientific lab. But Arthur McLain's place is just one of Altamira's cheap, cramped buildings.

"He really is a poor man," you say.

"The professor has given his life to the Amazon," Zillo answers. "He has not tried to grow rich, like all the others. He cares about the creatures no one else cares about."

"He isn't here," you say, noticing the big padlock on the door. "Where would he be?"

Zillo spots a couple of street kids. He speaks rapidly to them in Portuguese. They answer, pointing and gesturing.

"These boys say the professor left a short while ago in a big hurry," Zillo says. "They say an Indian came and banged on his door. Then they left."

"They've got to know where my grandpa is!" you say. "You said you could get us a boat. Let's go right now."

"No—not at night. There's too much danger."

"But McLain just left. If we go now, we can catch up."

Zillo scratches his bare toe in the dirt. "Okay," he says reluctantly. "I will get a bo

Turn to page

118

The jeep takes you to a neat white bungalow. The Brazilian cop leads you inside. A man in a pressed khaki shirt and aviator sunglasses sits in the center of the shady room at a polished desk. In the shadows stands a thin, elderly man.

Your grandfather stares in disbelief at the older man. "Arthur!" he exclaims. "Arthur McLain—is that you?"

The man steps forward. He is gaunt. He wears a pale, rumpled suit. Shyly, he smiles. "Hello, George," he says.

Your grandfather turns to you. "This is Dr. McLain, the biologist we've come to see. He's spent almost his whole life in the Amazon. He knows the pink dolphin better than anyone, except maybe the native Indians. But Arthur . . ." Your grandpa blinks. "Why are we in the police station?"

"George, this is Colonel Costa. Colonel, may I introduce Dr. George Coleman, the famous author and scientist."

The colonel nods and smiles thinly. Your grandpa introduces you too, but the policeman ignores you.

"Now, Dr. Coleman," Colonel Costa says, "I am told you've come to solve the mystery of the pink dolphins. I am sorry to disappoint you, but the mystery must not be solved."

Your grandpa turns to Arthur McLain. The old biologist nods.

"I'm sorry, George," he says, "but there's nothing we can do. Please let me explain why."

Turn to page 80.

Zillo raises his eyebrows and looks at you expectantly.

You swallow. "Well, we were wondering— what if Zillo came to the States with us? He could go to school with me. He has no other family, you know. He needs us."

Your grandfather smiles. "And the Amazon needs him. Yes, Zillo— come along. But I hope you'll come back here someday."

"I bet we'll all come back," you say. "There's a lot of work to do here."

"Yes," says your grandfather. "There sure is."

The End

ABOUT THE AUTHOR

DOUG WILHELM is the author of *The Forgotten Planet, Scene of the Crime,* and *The Secret of Mystery Hill* in Bantam's Choose Your Own Adventure series. A freelance writer and editor, he lives in Montpelier, Vermont, and has a son, Bradley, who is seven years old.

ABOUT THE ILLUSTRATOR

RON WING is a cartoonist and illustrator who has contributed to many publications. His Choose Your Own Adventure credits include *You Are a Millionaire, Skateboard Champion, The Island of Time, Vampire Invaders, Outlaw Gulch, The Forgotten Planet,* and *Everest Adventure!* Ron lives and works in Benton, Pennsylvania.